THIS BOOK BELONGS TO

PETTICOAT PIRATES

Petticoat
PIRATES

The Seahorses of Scallop Bay

ERICA-JANE WATERS

LITTLE, BROWN BOOKS FOR YOUNG READERS
www.lbkids.co.uk

LITTLE, BROWN BOOKS FOR YOUNG READERS

First published in Great Britain in 2013 by Little, Brown Books for Young Readers

Copyright © 2013 by Erica-Jane Waters

The moral right of Erica-Jane Waters to be identified as author
and illustrator has been asserted.

*All characters and events in this publication, other than those
clearly in the public domain, are fictitious and any resemblance
to real persons, living or dead, is purely coincidental.*

A CIP catalogue record for this book
is available from the British Library.

ISBN 978-1-907411-98-4

Typeset in Golden Cockerel by M Rules
Printed and bound in Great Britain by
Clays, St Ives plc

Papers used by LBYR are from well-managed forests
and other responsible sources.

MIX
Paper from
responsible sources
FSC® C104740
www.fsc.org

Little, Brown Books for Young Readers
An imprint of
Little, Brown Book Group
100 Victoria Embankment
London EC4Y 0DY

An Hachette UK Company
www.hachette.co.uk

www.lbkids.co.uk

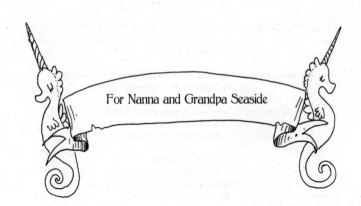

For Nanna and Grandpa Seaside

PERIWINKLE
LAGOON
AND THE SURROUNDING
SEAS

THE
PETTICOAT PIRATES

PERIWINKLE LAGOON

Contents

Prologue

Many morns ago, a small basket floated into Periwinkle Lagoon. Inside, under the shade of a tattered umbrella, were three baby girls!

Captainess Periwinkle, the leader of the pirates in the lagoon, raised the three babies until they were old enough to live on their own ship. They called it *The Petticoat*! When they moved on board, the girls each filled their cabins with their favourite things.

Marina wanted to be surrounded by paper,

pens and pencils. She placed a sturdy wooden drawing board by her bunk so that she could spend her time plotting maps and drawing pictures of sea creatures. She covered her cabin walls with her own paintings of beautiful seahorses. She kept lots of glass bottles on her shelves so that she could send letters to her friends the mermaids by popping them into the waves from her porthole.

Marina

Aqua stuffed her cabin to the beams with fabulous outfits. She moved all of her sparkling petticoats and skirts, frilly hats, boxes of bangles and other pirate treasure from the flagship to *The Petticoat*, even though the Captainess laughed at how many boat trips it took! She also put up a bookcase that covered a whole

wall, and packed it with hundreds of books about deep-sea beasties so that she could be the lagoon's resident expert.

Oceana designed her cabin to look like a science laboratory. She stacked her shelves with test tubes, Petri dishes and glass jars. She settled her microscope – a gift from the Captainess – on a desk beneath her porthole so that she would be able to study tiny sea creatures and

OCEANA

plants. She wanted to become a great inventor and make the pirates of the lagoon proud, so she filled boxes with all the tools and materials she would need.

The three pirates were a bit nervous to move on to their own ship away from the Captainess, but they quickly made *The Petticoat* feel like home. Little did they know what adventures lay ahead . . .

Chapter One

Autumn in Periwinkle Lagoon was Marina's favourite time of year. The trees that clung to the rocks around their watery home turned orange, red and purple and lots of different sea birds would arrive to roost before the winter. It was also the time of year when the annual Seahorse Gala was held! Marina loved the extra large seahorses that were specially trained to take a rider, especially Misty, a beautiful lavender-coloured seahorse the Captainess

had given Marina when she was just a nipper. Marina tried to practise her riding whenever she could, and this year she had finally been allowed to try out for the gala itself!

Each year pirates and sea creatures from across the seven seas would visit the lagoon to watch all the seahorse events from dancing to jumping. The most famous event of all was the grand race, which involved a lot of different and difficult skills. The prize for winning was the precious Ice Pearl Trophy, presented every year by the Ice King and Queen from the Northern Seas. Because the gala was so important, anyone who wanted to compete had to take part in a qualifying trial first to show the judges that their riding was good enough. Marina had just finished her trial and was heading back to *The Petticoat* to wait for the result. She was feeling

nervous but very excited – she and Misty had done some good jumping this morning!

Marina gazed up at the colourful leaves as she rowed her way back to *The Petticoat*.

All the ships apart from the flagship had been moved out of the lagoon and anchored in the open sea to allow the gala to take place within the sheltered rocky walls where the pirates usually lived.

"Throw me the rope ladder!" Marina called as she approached her ship. "I'm back!"

Her friends Aqua and Oceana quickly lowered the little ladder down the side of *The Petticoat*'s hull.

"How was the trial over in the lagoon? Did you get through?" Oceana asked in a rush.

"I don't know yet," Marina said as she hauled herself over the rails and on to the deck. "The sea-post gulls are delivering the results soon!"

"I know you'll get through," said Aqua. "You're the best seahorse rider I know!"

"Thank you," Marina replied. She smiled at her friend. "But there was some stiff competition there this year."

"Like who?" Aqua asked.

"Well," Marina continued, "there was a

new team from somewhere, and they jumped so high nobody could quite believe it!"

"Who were they?" said Aqua.

"It was hard to say," replied Marina. "I didn't recognise them. They had helmets and armour covering their bodies. They caused a bit of trouble actually."

"How so?" Oceana asked.

"The judges asked them lots of questions and seemed suspicious. I think they thought there might have been some magic involved – and you know that's strictly forbidden in the Seahorse Gala."

"Well it does sound suspicious to me," Aqua said, putting her hand on her hip. "How could anyone jump higher than you and Misty?"

Marina laughed. "You're too kind, Aqua! I think I still need to keep my pirate fingers

crossed that the judges thought my riding was good enough." She looked out at the silvery sea and the clouds that sailed past the low sun. The wind that blew gently through her dark hair carried a hint of a message.

"What is it, Marina?" asked Aqua. "Is the wind telling you something?" Marina was well known within Periwinkle Lagoon for her wind-whispering skills.

"No, no, it's probably nothing," Marina replied cheerfully. "It just sounds like something is coming ... "

A loud squawk and a flap of feathers interrupted Marina as a sea-post gull landed clumsily on *The Petticoat*'s rails.

"That will be what was coming!" Aqua scoffed as she took the rolled-up scroll from the bird's beak and handed it to Marina.

"Quickly! Open it!" said Oceana.

Marina untied the red bow and unrolled the creamy paper. "Dear Marina," she read aloud. "You have been successful in your trial. Your teammate will be Captainess Periwinkle.

We look forward to seeing you at the gala."
Marina gasped and rested a hand on her chest.
"I'm competing alongside the Captainess! I'm so
proud I could burst!"

Suddenly, they heard the warning bells
ringing out from the flagship. Marina quickly
rolled her scroll back up and stuck it in her belt.

"Limpets!" Aqua cried. "What's happening?"

"Listen," said Marina as she counted the
rhythm and tune of the bells. "It's the jellyfish
warning!"

"Don't be silly, you must be wrong," Aqua
snipped. "There are never any jellyfish around
Periwinkle Lagoon in autumn!"

"But it's definitely the jellyfish warning,"
Marina continued. "We need to make sure
Misty and the other seahorses are OK over at
the stables."

Quickly the three pirates flung on their cloaks and climbed down into their little rowing boat.

"There wasn't a jellyfish in sight when I was at the trial earlier," Marina said, rowing the girls back into the lagoon's still waters.

Oceana gasped and pointed over the side of the boat into the cold silvery water.

The three pirates stared down into the waves around them. The waters  of Periwinkle Lagoon were thick with h u n d r e d s of stinging jellyfish!

Chapter Two

"It's hard work pushing the oars past these jellyfish," said Marina as she rowed the little boat through the thick shoal of slimy creatures to the seahorse paddocks. A wall of coral and tall driftwood fencing protected the seahorses and kept them safe from harm.

"It looks like the jellyfish haven't been able to get in," Oceana said. She stood up carefully in the prow of the boat to unlatch the gate.

"These particular jellyfish are especially

poisonous!" Aqua shuddered, looking at their trailing pink stingers. "It is extremely peculiar to find them here at this time of year. The waters are far too cold. There's definitely something fishy going on!"

"Don't you mean *jelly*fishy?" Marina giggled.

"Look," said Oceana, pointing over to the little stables that were lined up along the cliff face.

"It's Captainess Periwinkle."

Closing the driftwood gate firmly behind them, the girls rowed over to find out what was going on.

The Captainess was with two of her officials in the royal rowing boats. They were just guiding Misty into her stable along with two other seahorses – Pearl and Coral – and securing the door.

18

"Ah, Petticoat Pirates!" the Captainess shouted across the paddock. "Come hither, me hearties, come hither! We have a most sticky situation on our hands!"

"What is it, Captainess?" Marina asked anxiously. "Is Misty all right? Has she been stung?"

"No, no, my little worry whelk, all the seahorses are well protected from jellyfish within this paddock. The coral walls go all the way to the seabed and the driftwood fencing is strong and secure."

"Why do you think the jellyfish are here, Captainess?" asked Aqua. "I've only ever seen them during the summer months before ..."

Captainess Periwinkle stared out at her lagoon and to the seas beyond. She had a worried look in her eyes. "This is no natural

20

event," she said, leaning closer to the three girls. "This, me hearties, is magic!"

The Petticoat Pirates looked at one another.

"M-m-magic?" Oceana stuttered. "I don't like jellyfish at the best of times, let alone magical jellyfish!"

"Someone has sent these jellyfish to disrupt our gala," Captainess Periwinkle continued. "The seahorses and their riders can't compete in infested waters – they will all be stung!"

"And these jellyfish are especially nasty ones," said Aqua, one eyebrow raised. "One single sting from their long pink tentacles

would make a grown pirate as paralysed as a plank for a week!"

"Well, we need to sort this problem out fast." Captainess Periwinkle wrung her hands together. "The reputation of our lagoon is at risk, young pirates! We have sea people travelling from the far reaches of the oceans. They are expecting the biggest and most spectacular gala these seas have ever seen! I'll look as foolish as a flapper fish if I have to cancel it."

Marina leant over the edge of her boat and stroked Misty's neck. "Does anyone have a reason to want to disrupt the gala?" she asked the Captainess.

"Well, earlier today at the trial we had a problem with some cheating. We had to disqualify a team from Scallop Bay."

"I've heard of Scallop Bay!" Aqua said. "That's where the Jellyfish Queen and her people live!"

Oceana turned as pale as a beluga whale. "J-J-Jellyfish Queen?" she stuttered.

"Yes," Aqua continued. "Was it the Jellyfish people who were disqualified, Captainess?"

"It's hard to tell ye – they were dressed head to toe in armour," she replied.

"We could take a closer look at one of the jellyfish to see if that throws up any more clues," Oceana suggested quietly while staring through her mother-of-pearl-rimmed glasses at her shoes.

"What an excellent idea!" said the Captainess. "You clever little clam!"

Oceana blushed a little and stared even harder at her buckled shoes.

"My Petticoat Pirates, if you can prove for me that it is the Jellyfish people who are responsible for this magic I would be for ever grateful. The gala has gone ahead without a glitch for more than three hundred pirate years, and we must not let it be ruined," said the Captainess.

The girls agreed to do everything they could to help. They rowed back to *The Petticoat* as quickly as they could through the sea of bobbing jellyfish.

"Wow," Aqua said as she and Marina climbed the ladder back on board *The Petticoat*. "These things are incredible – look at their tentacles!"

"Here," Marina said, passing Aqua a large glass jar. "Lower this down to Oceana."

"I think they're rather beautiful." Oceana carefully lifted one of the smaller jellyfish

out of the lagoon with the oar of the rowing boat. She plopped it into the large jar that was now full of seawater.

Marina and Aqua helped Oceana over the rails of the ship. "We need to take this specimen down to my cabin for analysis," Oceana said, opening the hatch which led below deck. "Are you two coming?"

"I'm right behind you!" Aqua said, nodding her blonde hair frantically. "There's nothing I like better than a beast from the deep. Though I'm not sure that we'll see anything other than jellyfish slime ..."

Marina smiled at her friend. "You might be right, but we must at least try to find out who has cast this magic so we can fix it in time for the gala."

The three girls entered Oceana's cabin and set the jar down on her research table. Oceana took a sea-cotton bud and gently wiped it along the jellyfish before placing it on a slide and under her microscope.

"Do you see anything?" asked Marina.

"She'll see slime," Aqua said, twiddling a strand of her long blonde hair around her finger.

"Oh, limpets, how frustrating," Oceana whispered under her breath. "I was hoping to see something unusual but there's nothing here except—"

"Slime?" Aqua said.

The three girls giggled.

Oceana put on her magnifying glasses and shone a torch inside the jar. "Nope, nothing unusual here at all, just a plain old jellyfish."

Marina looked out of Oceana's porthole window to see the sun dipping below the horizon. "The sun sets so early now," she said, glancing at her pocket watch.

"It's high time I put a fish pie in the oven!" Aqua said, her tummy rumbling.

The three hungry pirates began to make their way out of Oceana's cabin and back up to the main deck where the living cabin was.

"Wait!" cried Oceana as she went to close her door behind her. "Look!"

Marina and Aqua both turned their heads. As darkness was falling upon the lagoon something strange was happening to the jellyfish in the jar.

"What IS that?" Marina murmured as the three girls edged closer to the table.

There, glowing bright pink in the jellyfish's body, was the shape of a scallop shell.

"I recognise that shell design," Aqua said, her forehead creasing. "It's definitely the emblem of the Jellyfish people of Scallop Bay. I remember seeing it in my book *Sea People from Afar*."

"Well remembered, Aqua," Marina said to her friend.

"So, what else do you know about the Jellyfish people?" asked Oceana, feeling herself shake ever so slightly in her shoes.

"They live at Scallop Bay and are ruled by a Queen named Olinda," Aqua replied. "They are very private and never leave Scallop Bay Island.

It seems very unusual that they should want to compete in our gala."

"How strange," Marina said, her milky-white face creased in confusion. "I wonder why they suddenly decided to venture away from their home."

"What's Scallop Bay Island like?" Oceana asked.

"No one ever visits as the shores are lined with dark, damp forests full of salt spiders which protect the Jellyfish Queen's castle!" Aqua replied.

"Limpets," squeaked Oceana.

"Well, to Scallop Bay we must go!" Marina said, disappearing into her own cabin and re-emerging a second later with an armful of rolled-up maps.

"Double limpets," Oceana squeaked again.

"Come on, we can plan our route over dinner," Marina continued as she climbed up the ladder on to the main deck. "We're going to need all our strength if we're going to be facing an evil Jellyfish Queen and her salt spiders!"

Chapter Three

With the sun well set and the large orangey moon rising in the night sky, the three girls tucked into a hearty fish pie.

"So . . ." Oceana began, nervously pushing a prawn around her plate. "What do the Jellyfish people look like?"

"I've never seen one in real life, nor has any pirate I know! But there's a pretty good description in my *Sea People from Afar* book," said Aqua.

Oceana turned to look at Aqua. "Are they . . ."

"Scary?" Aqua replied with her mouth full. "Oh yes, they're scary all right!"

"Aqua!" Marina said in a warning tone, seeing the expression on Oceana's face.

"Well, they're not going to be winning any beauty contests, trust me!" Aqua said. "They have arms and legs like you and I, but MUCH bigger and MUCH longer and MUCH slimier."

Oceana held her spoonful of pie in front of her open mouth, frozen with fear.

"They have bodies just like us, but instead of wearing clothes they wear scaly armour made from electric eel scales," Aqua went on.

"And what about their heads?" asked Oceana, her voice shaking.

"Well," Aqua said, leaning forward, "that's the weird bit. Instead of heads like you and I, they have ... jellyfish heads!"

"Suddenly I'm not so hungry," Oceana said, dropping her spoonful of fish pie back on to her plate. She stood up to start clearing the table, then suggested in a quiet voice: "Maybe I could just stay here while you go to Scallop Bay Island?"

"But, Oceana, we can't do it without you!" Marina said. She lifted up one of her maps which were spread on one side of the table. "Looking at this map of Scallop Bay, I think we're going to have to find our way by seahorse once we get to the island. We'll need your skills to build some armour to protect us and our seahorses from jellyfish stings! Do you think you could help?"

"Yes, I can do that," Oceana replied, managing a small smile. "I think I've got the right kind of materials in my cabin." Oceana was well known for her inventions, and she always had lots of tools at hand on the ship. She disappeared below deck to build the armour in her cabin.

"And what can I do?" Aqua asked.

"You can help me with the washing up!" said Marina. "I always like *The Petticoat* to be ship shape before an adventure!"

"Aye aye, Captain," Aqua joked as she jumped up and began to fill the sink with soapy water.

Chapter Four

Very early the next morn, all was ready for the Petticoat Pirates to set off on their adventure to Scallop Bay Island. Oceana had worked late into the night to build three sets of armour for the seahorses and one each for her, Marina and Aqua.

"I'm just writing a note to let the Captainess know of our plan," Aqua said, scrawling a message on to a scrap of paper and then whistling for a sea-post gull.

"Excellent idea," Marina said. "We must hurry over to the seahorse stables to prepare Misty, Pearl and Coral in their armour." She and Oceana began loading up their rowing boat. "These suits are incredible, Oceana!"

"Thank you," Oceana said, her sand-coloured eyes flickering with pride. "I used

some of my finest metal, and they're riveted with black pearls, the strongest you'll find anywhere in the seas."

A sea-post gull suddenly swooped over their heads and landed on the ship's rail. Aqua quickly popped her note to the Captainess in the gull's satchel and climbed down to join the others in the boat. "Let's hurry!" she cried. "We need to get to Scallop Bay and solve this mystery before the gala is due to begin!"

When they arrived at the stables, the three pirates lifted the lightweight armour on to the seahorses. The metal would protect their skin and shimmering scales from the jellyfish's poisonous stings!

"Wow, they look fabulous!" gushed Aqua. "I love the pearls, Oceana!"

Marina and Oceana shared a smile – their friend was crazy about fashion, no matter what the situation!

"Which seahorse should I ride?" Aqua asked.

"I think you would be a perfect match with Pearl," Marina replied. "She is a very sensible and cautious seahorse. With your feisty and fearless nature, you two will be an excellent team!"

Pearl was smaller than Marina's seahorse, Misty, but just as fast a swimmer. She had the

milkiest white skin, which shimmered pink all over just like a real pearl.

"Limpets," Oceana muttered, shaking her chestnut hair. "That means I'm riding Coral!"

"Don't worry." Marina put her hand gently on Oceana's arm. "I know Coral looks big, but her strength and speed will work well for you."

"Are you sure?" Oceana still looked nervous. "I haven't had much riding practice."

"Look!" Marina laughed. "She likes you!" The golden seahorse was looking at Oceana with big, wide eyes, her scales sparkling in the morning sun.

"I'm not sure she'll like me that much when I have to ride her," Oceana mumbled. But she was quickly distracted by the arrival of a sea-post gull landing next to her in the boat.

"It must be a note from Captainess Periwinkle!" said Marina. She opened the scroll and read aloud:

> My dear Petticoat Pirates,
> I have just read of yer plan to visit
> Scallop Bay Island. Brave souls ye be
> and I'm as grateful as a mollusc in
> mud to yer.
> Take much care, me hearties.
> Captainess Periwinkle

The sea-post gull flew off through the cold morning sky back towards the flagship and the girls quickly rowed to *The Petticoat* with the seahorses swimming alongside. Oceana's armour seemed to be working perfectly in the jellyfish-filled waters.

Back on board, they made haste to leave for Scallop Bay Island. Aqua let down the sails and Oceana hoisted up the anchor. "Anchors aweigh!" they cried.

"Anchors aweigh!" Marina called back as she took the helm. The chilly autumn wind whipped around her ink-black hair, whispering to her of the dangers that lay ahead.

She watched as Aqua and Oceana turned the sails to meet the wind, and thanked her lucky sea stars that she had such good friends. Together they would save their little lagoon from the bad magic that threatened their Seahorse Gala, no matter what.

Chapter Five

Chilly green waves crashed against the bow of *The Petticoat* as it made its way through the seas.

"Keep those sails loose," Marina called to Aqua and Oceana, "we don't want to go too fast. Remember our seahorses are tethered to the side."

Oceana fastened the main sail so it didn't catch too much wind. Then she skipped up to the poop deck where Marina was steering the ship.

"Do you think the seahorses will need a break soon, Marina?" Oceana asked.

"Yes, you're right," Marina replied, looking at her pocket watch. "They've been swimming alongside the ship for a long time now. Let's drop anchor and rest a while."

As soon as *The Petticoat* had come safely to a halt, Marina, Aqua and Oceana picked up a bucket of delicious ocean oats and climbed

down to their rowing boat. The three hungry seahorses swam over to the girls, eager to see what was for lunch.

"One at a time, one at a time!" Marina struggled to hold the bucket steady as the three big seahorses nuzzled and chomped.

"May I try?" Oceana asked nervously.

"Of course!" Marina said, handing the bucket to her kind friend. "But don't let go!"

Oceana laughed as the beautiful seahorses pushed their long snouts into the bucket and looked up at her with their big eyes. She loved animals very much, but was a little nervous of such large sea creatures.

"I've got just the thing for dessert!" Aqua said. Her bracelets jangled as she rummaged around in the pocket of her long, flowing cloak.

"Is there anything you *don't* have in your pockets?" Marina giggled.

"Always good to be prepared," Aqua replied, pulling out a little pink spotty bag.

"Sea sugar cubes!" Oceana beamed. "May I have one?"

"Not before we've had our lunch," Aqua said, "and besides, these are especially for our seahorse friends, to say thank you for coming and helping us on our mission."

Pearl moved closer to Aqua and nuzzled her snout into her arm, trying to get at the cubes.

"Give me a chance!" Aqua quickly placed a cube flat on her hand and held it out first to

Pearl, before doing the same to Coral and then Misty.

Suddenly, Marina's tummy rumbled loudly. "I guess it's our lunchtime too! Aqua, what's on the menu for us today?" Aqua was *The Petticoat*'s cook – she made nearly all of the yummy meals that the three pirates enjoyed.

"Octopus and sea potato stew," Aqua replied with a grin. "I thought it would be perfect for such a chilly autumn day."

The girls gave the seahorses one last sea sugar cube each then climbed back up on board and into the main cabin.

As Aqua stirred the pot of stew, Marina rolled out one of her hand-drawn maps on the

table and used a seashell to hold down each corner.

"So, how far is it from here?" Aqua asked.

"It's not too far at all, and the journey should be nice and simple. Well, at least until we reach the island and then it might be trickier! Do you have any books about Scallop Bay, Aqua?"

"I think we know enough already!" Oceana

cried. "Salt spiders, giant jellyfish-headed people and an evil Queen!"

"I know you're frightened," Marina said, placing her hands on Oceana's shoulders, "but no matter how frightening something is it's always best to be prepared. Being armed with knowledge is far more powerful than any sword."

"I agree," Aqua said, "but I'll still be taking a very sharp and very pointy narwhal sword with me just in case my knowledge doesn't help against a giant salt spider!" She turned down the heat on the stew and searched in a pile of books on the sideboard. "I'm sure I left *Sea People from Afar* in here yesterday ... Aha! Here we are."

Aqua brought the heavy book to the table and flopped through the pages until she reached the chapter about the Jellyfish people.

53

"That must be the Jellyfish Queen's castle," Marina said. She peered at a painting of a turreted building that was perched on top of a tall mountain, surrounded by mists and forest.

"Look," Aqua said, pointing to the opposite page, "this is what the Jellyfish people look like." An illustration of a long-limbed being with a jellyfish-shaped head and tendrils stared back at them.

"What's that scary-looking thing it's wearing?" Oceana asked.

"Oh that. That's its armour. They may look big and scary but their jelly heads are very

delicate. They wear special armour to protect them," Aqua replied. "Personally I wouldn't wear it in that colour but I suppose Jellyfish people have their own sense of style."

Aqua turned the page and the three pirates' mouths dropped open at the painting before them.

Oceana stepped back. "Limpets … is that …?"

" … Queen Olinda," Marina finished her friend's sentence.

The painting on the page was so lifelike the girls felt as though Olinda, the Queen of the Jellyfish people, was in the room with them. She was pictured holding a whalebone bow

and arrow. Her arms and legs were extremely long and although she had eyes, a nose and a mouth, her head was large and just like a jellyfish's. Instead of hair she had long tentacles that swept down to the ground.

"Actually, she doesn't look *that* scary," Aqua said, spooning three portions of stew into little shell bowls.

"She does to me!" said Oceana.

"Do you know anything else about the Jellyfish people?" Marina asked Aqua as she rolled up her maps to make room for dinner.

"Not a lot, I'm afraid! They're so private, I don't think anyone else has ever set foot on the island before." Aqua set the bowls of stew down in front of her friends.

"It doesn't make sense to me," Oceana said, frowning. "Why suddenly decide to take part in

an event with hundreds of spectators if you're so shy and private? And then cheat?"

"They didn't even deny it," Marina said. "They just turned around and went back to Scallop Bay." She turned another page and gasped. "Salt spiders!"

Oceana dropped her spoon and muttered a faint "Limpets!" under her breath.

"Ah, yes! Salt spiders," Aqua said, shaking her head. "We want to avoid them as much as possible."

Marina ran her finger along the text underneath the picture of a large, white spider.

"Salt spiders are found exclusively in and around the forests of Scallop Bay in the Northern Seas. They have a leg span of one hundred and twenty centimetres and their webs are strong enough to hold a small ship.

They are extremely sensitive to bright light, which makes the dark, damp forests of Scallop Bay the perfect home for them."

The three girls looked at one another with wide eyes.

"We should get moving again," Marina said, looking out of the porthole. "The sun never stays long in the sky at this time of year and we don't want to arrive in the dark."

So *The Petticoat* set sail again, the three seahorses swimming alongside it, heading to the mist-shrouded shores of Scallop Bay.

Chapter Six

It wasn't long before *The Petticoat* neared the shores of Scallop Bay Island.

"I can see it up ahead," Oceana shouted down from the crow's nest as she looked

through her telescope. "It's so misty I can barely make it out, but there is land ahoy."

"We can't go any further by boat," said Marina. "We should change into our armour now and press ahead on the seahorses."

Aqua lowered the anchor while Oceana fetched the suits of armour from below deck.

The girls dressed themselves quietly, all feeling anxious about the task that lay ahead in spite of the protective layers they'd be wearing. Marina folded up a map of the bay and island and put it in her shoulder bag. "Come on, pirates, let's go and face the Jellyfish Queen. We can't let anybody stand in the way of our gala!"

"Wait! We've forgotten something," Aqua said, dashing into the main cabin. "Here, catch!" she shouted as she came back out. She tossed

narwhal swords to Marina and Oceana before fastening one to her own belt.

"Good thinking," Marina said as she climbed down the rope ladder and mounted Misty. "We may need to cut our way through the spiderwebs and the thick forest."

"Limpets," Oceana squeaked as she fell clumsily from the rope ladder and landed back to front on Coral's saddle.

Finally with Aqua in Pearl's saddle and Oceana facing the right way around, the three Petticoat Pirates began riding through the misty sea towards the island.

"Limpets," Oceana murmured as she

looked down at scores of jellyfish blobbing around her armoured legs. The jellyfish's stingers brushed against the pirates and the seahorses, but their poisonous tentacles couldn't get past Oceana's clever armour design.

"There should be a small inlet somewhere around here according to the map," Marina said. She pulled on Misty's reins to guide him left.

"There!" shouted Oceana from the back of the group. "I can see it."

Steadily the seahorses and their riders swam up the swampy inlet and deep into the forest that lined the shore. The trees grew right out of the water and the whole place was blanketed in fog, making it very, very dark.

"Thank goodness we came by seahorse," Marina said, patting the side of Misty's neck. "We could never have squeezed our rowing boat through here – the forest is far too thick."

Strange chatters and squawks echoed around their ears.

"This place is too creepy, I don't like it one

bit!" Oceana said. She had her arms wrapped tightly around Coral's neck.

"That's the idea!" Aqua snapped. "The Jellyfish people want to keep outsiders, well, outside! You're not supposed to want to come on holiday here!"

"Aqua, why don't you cut us a path through that way?" Marina asked, wanting to ease the tension between her friends. "You'll get to use your narwhal sword." Marina smiled at Oceana who still clung to her seahorse, her eyes barely open.

"Well that's the most sensible thing anyone's said in a long time." Aqua began hacking at the long tree branches that were draped across their path. "I still haven't seen any spiderwebs yet – I reckon those salt spiders are just a story to try and scare people away!"

But just as the words left Aqua's mouth, something large and white and leggy dropped down from the tree branches above.

"Heeeeeeeelp!" Aqua screamed as the large salt spider wrapped her up in its web.

Marina and Oceana watched in horror as the spider spun Aqua around and around into a bundle of silk. Then, with their friend on its hairy back, it scuttled off up the tree into the darkness above.

"Aqua!" Marina shouted. "Aqua, where are you?"

"Oh, limpets," Oceana said. She took a deep breath and jumped off Coral, on to the tree the spider had run up.

"Oceana!" Marina gasped. "What are you *doing*?"

But Oceana had no time to reply as she

hurried up the tree branches as if they were the rigging aboard *The Petticoat*.

Marina watched as her shy and timid friend disappeared up into the darkness. What should she do now? But after a moment – which felt more like four-score years to Marina – a great flash of light blazed in the treetops above her head.

"A flare!" Marina whispered to herself. "Oceana, you clever little catfish, you've set off a flare."

As the flare lit up the tree canopy above, Marina could see a thick tangle of salt spiderwebs draped all along the tops of the trees. There was Aqua, caught tight in a cocoon of silk! Dozens of spiders were scuttling away from the bright light as Oceana climbed the branches to reach her friend.

Marina could do nothing but hold her breath and keep the seahorses still as she watched Oceana try to cut Aqua free. But the light of the flare soon began to fade and Marina could see the large spiders making their way back to her friends!

"Oceana, light another flare! They're coming back!" she shouted.

Oceana struck another flare and once again the white, hairy spiders scuttled away. Finally, just as the second flare began to fade, Aqua wriggled free and the two friends quickly climbed back down the tree and remounted their seahorses.

"Oh, Oceana," Aqua said, panting, "you just saved my life! That is the bravest thing anyone has ever done for me – thank you!"

"Oh, don't thank me," Oceana said, turning

a little bit pink. "It was something Marina said that gave me the courage to do it."

Marina and Aqua both looked at Oceana with their eyebrows raised.

"Well," she continued, "you said that knowledge was more powerful than any sword. We learnt from Aqua's book that salt spiders hate bright light, so I packed a few flares in my bag."

"What would we do without you and your clever brain?" Marina said, taking Misty's reins once more. "Come on, let's hurry out of this place before another of us gets snatched by a spider! If we carry on along this way we should soon reach Queen Olinda's castle."

Chapter Seven

Soon the watery forest floor became shallower, making it difficult for the seahorses to swim through. The trees had thinned out too, and rays of hazy light shone down from the white sky above.

"I think we're going to have to continue on foot," said Marina. She poked her narwhal sword past a few jellyfish and down into the water to test the depth. "We'll have to tether Misty, Pearl and Coral here and collect them on the way back."

The girls jumped down and quickly tied the seahorses' reins to a tree. Aqua hung up a sack of ocean oats for them to graze on.

"You wait here until we get back," Oceana said, stroking Coral's neck. The seahorse gently rubbed her snout on Oceana's arm. "It's too light for salt spiders in this part of the forest – you'll be safe here."

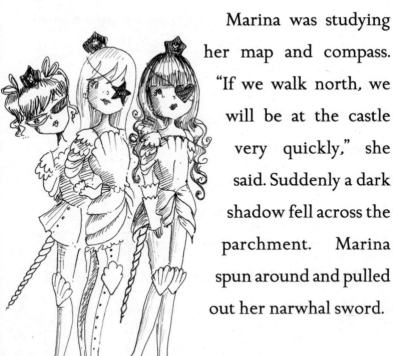

Marina was studying her map and compass. "If we walk north, we will be at the castle very quickly," she said. Suddenly a dark shadow fell across the parchment. Marina spun around and pulled out her narwhal sword.

"What brings you here, stranger?" a deep voice bellowed.

Marina, Aqua and Oceana were confronted by two tall Jellyfish people who looked, judging by their armour and whalebone bows and arrows, like they were some sort of royal guards.

"We are the Petticoat Pirates from Periwinkle Lagoon," Marina said loudly, even though she was shaking inside.

"Ah, Periwinkle Lagoon!" said the tallest of the

guards. He leant forward, his tentacles billowing behind him.

"We would like to speak with Queen Olinda," Aqua said. She stepped forward and stood on her tiptoes, trying to make herself seem taller.

"Queen Olinda doesn't like visitors," the Jellyfish guard said in a slithery voice.

"Well, the Periwinkle Lagoon Seahorse Gala doesn't like cheaters!" Oceana burst out. Then she gasped and put her hands over her mouth.

"Cheaters? Cheaters!" The guard moved close to Oceana. "The Jellyfish people of Scallop Bay Island are NOT cheaters."

Oceana stood frozen with fear as the creature slowly moved away again.

"Very well!" he continued. "We will take

you to the castle, but don't expect a warm welcome from our Queen. You will see that we are not cheaters."

The guards took the Petticoat Pirates by the arms and marched them out of the swampy forest towards the castle.

After a steep climb up a narrow track, Queen Olinda's castle came into view. Built from black stone, it had more turrets than the girls could count, some of which were disappearing into the dark swirling clouds in the sky above.

The pirates were led through the heavy castle doors and into a vast hall. Its vaulted ceiling stretched up as far as the eye could see, and there was a black iron staircase in the centre. Salty water dripped down the stone walls and formed puddles on the floor.

"Limpets," Oceana whimpered, wishing

she and her friends were back at home in Periwinkle Lagoon rather than in an evil Jellyfish Queen's castle.

"Wait here," the tall guard said as he ushered to the others to let go of the girls' arms. "I will announce your arrival to Queen Olinda."

Marina, Aqua and Oceana huddled together while they waited.

"What are you going to say to Queen Olinda?" Oceana asked Marina nervously.

"I'm not sure," Marina replied. "But on the walk here, the winds whispered that there may be some truth in what the Jellyfish people are saying."

"You mean they didn't cheat?" Aqua said.

"I don't know, but I feel there is more to this than we think."

"Listen, what's that noise?" Oceana whispered. "It sounds like . . . a waterfall!"

The girls looked up at the iron staircase and watched as a torrent of water gushed down the steps, flooding the hall with even more puddles. There, at the top of the stairs, stood two towering figures. The girls watched openmouthed as the two Jellyfish people glided down the stairs.

"Are they . . . ?" Oceana began, amazed.

". . . Floating!" Aqua finished, just as stunned.

The tall Jellyfish people seemed to hover effortlessly over the steps. "I am Queen Olinda," said one.

Her limbs were long just like they had been painted in Aqua's book, but she was far more beautiful than the picture. She wore a

long translucent gown that flashed pink and purple along its edging, just like a jellyfish. Her tentacles flowed elegantly behind her as she drew closer to the girls.

"And this is my sister Luna," the Queen continued.

"And we are the—" Marina began.

"I know who you are and why you have come," Luna said suddenly, pushing her sister aside and glaring at Marina. "You pirates have done us a great injustice."

Marina stepped forward. "Please, Queen Olinda, may I ask why you have sent a shoal of stinging jellyfish to disrupt the gala? I understand that your seahorse team must have been disappointed but that's no reason to—"

"Why should the gala go ahead if we are not allowed to take part?" Luna interrupted again, her long arms folded in front of her.

The Petticoat Pirates looked at one another nervously.

"Because your seahorse jumping team was using magic to jump higher, and that's against the rules," Marina said cautiously. She didn't want to cause any more upset than they already had.

"We are not cheaters," Queen Olinda said softly from behind her bossy sister.

"Then why didn't you explain that to the officials at Periwinkle Lagoon?" Marina asked.

Queen Olinda didn't reply, but just turned away and hung her head.

"We don't have to explain anything to you pirates!" Luna snapped, before storming off back up the stairs and disappearing from view.

The three Petticoat Pirates stood in silence, wondering what to do next.

"We are a very private and very proud race," Queen Olinda eventually said, turning back to face the pirates. "And things have been very difficult here at Scallop Bay Island since I was made Queen. Come with me, and I will explain."

Queen Olinda led the girls through the castle and out into the gardens. A long rectangular pond stretched out in front of them filled with tiny delicate jellyfish in shades of pink and purple and electric blue. Around the pond grew exotic flowers that seemed to glow – the pirates had never seen anything like them before. Queen Olinda picked a bright blue rose from a bush and fastened it to her dress.

"Here at Scallop Bay Island we are very keen seahorse riders, but as we are such a private people, we never usually compete in races." Queen Olinda, Marina, Aqua and Oceana walked through an archway at the end of the pond and a seahorse stables and paddock appeared in front of them.

"Wow," Aqua whispered as the three pirates admired the many strong seahorses and their riders.

"So why did you decide to come to the trial for our gala this year?" Marina asked.

"Just recently our parents passed away and I was made Queen much sooner than I expected. My younger sister Luna hasn't

been coping very well. She misses our parents terribly, and she hates the idea of following my rules. She is not like the rest of us here at Scallop Bay Island – she wanted to show the rest of the seas how good we were at seahorse riding. I thought that if I agreed to compete, it would help to make her happy, but it has made things so much worse."

Just then, a large seahorse and his rider jumped right over their heads and sploshed back down into the training paddock.

"My people were very much against us going out to the gala. They were nervous and certain we would bring trouble upon ourselves. But I was desperate for my sister to have something she wanted."

"So you didn't cheat – you really are very skilled seahorse riders?" Marina asked gently.

"Yes," replied Queen Olinda.

"So," Oceana said, shuffling forward, "why didn't you tell the gala officials all this?"

"Because Luna was so angry! I had to get us back here to Scallop Bay Island before we brought any more embarrassment on ourselves. And now I'm not very popular with my people as we are thought of as cheats. I wish I had put my foot down with Luna and never gone in the first place." Queen Olinda stroked a seahorse's neck that had come up to nuzzle. "I am a terrible ruler and a hopeless Queen. I should have known that leaving our lovely island would lead to disaster."

"I have an idea about how we can fix things," said Marina. "But it would mean returning to Periwinkle Lagoon to compete in the gala. Do you think you could?"

"But we have been disqualified. I don't see how the gala officials would agree," the Queen said. "And besides, Luna is too angry."

"It'll be OK. I can send word ahead that you and your team will compete – but on Periwinkle Lagoon seahorses. You can't perform magic on someone else's seahorses, so that will prove you are not cheats!" Marina said, her dark eyes glistening with excitement.

"And you are the Queen, Olinda," Oceana said shyly. "You have the power to make the decisions and take responsibility for your people. You must stand up to your sister, no matter how angry she may be. You are the Queen of the Jellyfish people."

The Queen stared out at her beautiful garden for a few moments.

"Very well, I will accept your offer of help in order to clear our names. I will inform my sister and my people of my decision."

"There's one other thing," Marina added. "What about the jellyfish shoal that has infested our lagoon?"

"That sounds like Luna's work – I will lift her magic right away."

Queen Olinda moved closer to Marina and rested her long hand on her arm. "Thank you, Marina. I will meet you in the bay in an hour."

Chapter Eight

Marina, Aqua and Oceana returned to where Misty, Pearl and Coral were waiting patiently. They were accompanied by six royal guards to protect them from the salt spiders as they made their way through the dark forest and back to the bay.

"We will join you at your ship shortly," the tallest guard said to Marina before turning back and disappearing between the trees.

"I don't know about you two," Aqua said

as she rode Pearl out towards *The Petticoat,* "but I'll be as glad as a gillyglipper to be back aboard our ship!"

Once they were safely on deck, Marina whistled for a sea-post gull and sat down to write a note to the Captainess.

Dear Captainess Periwinkle,
There has been a terrible
misunderstanding about the team from
Scallop Bay Island. I am certain that
they did not cheat at all during the
trials.
  I have suggested that they take
part in the gala and ride on Periwinkle
Lagoon seahorses to prove they are
competing fairly.
  Queen Olinda has lifted the magic

that infested our lagoon with poisonous jellyfish, so they should disappear very soon.

Please send word if you would be so gracious as to grant your permission for this to happen.

Your pirate daughter,

Marina

She popped the letter into the sea-post gull's satchel and sent him on his way.

"Look, Marina, look!" Oceana and Aqua shrieked from the ship's rails.

Marina turned to where her friends were pointing. From around the side of the bay sailed the grandest galleon that any of the young pirates had ever seen. Its sails shimmered pink and purple. The ship had three grand masts and

its sides were delicately carved with jellyfish patterns. Standing at the bow of the grand ship was Queen Olinda, dressed in her finest gown and shiniest armour.

Marina noticed a large flag that was flapping in the wind from the front mast. "The Scallop Bay emblem," she whispered to

herself. "Just like the pattern we saw on the jellyfish."

Queen Olinda's grand galleon sailed through the choppy seas following *The Petticoat* – along with Misty, Pearl and Coral – back to Periwinkle Lagoon.

A little squawk from the ship's rails alerted Marina to another sea-post gull. The three girls huddled around the reply from their Captainess and Marina read the letter aloud. It had been written on the flagship's headed paper.

Me hearties,

It sounds like you've had to be the bravest of pirates on your adventure to Scallop Bay Island. I would expect nothing less, but am as grateful as a shark in a shoal of sardines to yer.

I am happy to tell you that the shoal of jellyfish has cleared from the lagoon so the gala can go ahead. What a mighty relief!

I am pleased that you believe the Jellyfish people did not use magic. Please let Queen Olinda know they are welcome to compete should they wish to. We will ask no questions as long as they take part fairly.

Your loving Captainess Periwinkle

94

"Excellent!" Marina sighed before placing the letter back into the sea-post gull's satchel.

"Please take this letter and pass it to Queen Olinda. She is on the galleon following us." Marina pointed to the grand ship, and the sea-post gull flapped off again.

As the two ships arrived back at Periwinkle Lagoon the sun was setting over the chilly seas. They dropped anchor outside the lagoon along with all the other ships that had arrived for the gala. It looked like there would be hundreds and hundreds of spectators for the coming events!

The three Petticoat Pirates were soon ready to retire to their cabins for the night. Tomorrow was to be an important and nerve-wracking day. With all the excitement and adventure at Scallop Bay Island, Marina had

almost forgotten that she was competing in the gala herself the very next morn!

She gave her riding boots a final polish, brushed down her jacket then climbed into her bunk before falling into a restless sleep.

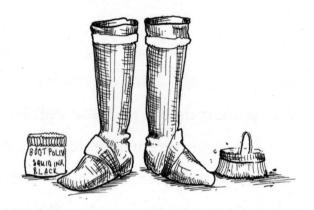

Chapter Nine

It was the morning of the gala and Marina,
Aqua and Oceana were up before dawn. Aqua
lit the little wood burner in the main cabin and
scrambled some eggs for breakfast. She laid out
three oyster-shell dishes and three mother-
of-pearl mugs. There was
a hot pot of kelp tea
steaming away on the hob
and the cabin felt cosy and
warm.

"Wow," Aqua gasped as Marina entered the cabin dressed in all her fancy gala outfit. "You look fabulous!"

"Thank you," she replied. "I feel so honoured to be competing alongside Captainess Periwinkle."

Oceana stumbled through the cabin door, still half asleep. "Limpets, this is very early in the morning," she moaned.

Marina laughed. "It's so nice that you've got out of your comfy bed to support me, Oceana. And Aqua, something smells delicious!"

"Well, the Seahorse Gala requires a lot of energy," Aqua said, dolloping scrambled egg on to the plates. "Sit down and eat. These eggs were fresh from the Periwinkle Deli this morn."

As the three pirates tucked into their yummy breakfast a voice came from outside the cabin: "Marina, Marina!"

"Captainess Periwinkle," Marina cried, jumping up from the table to hug the Captainess as she strode through the door.

Captainess Periwinkle was dressed in a fitted sea-tweed jacket with tiny pearl buttons all the way down the front. She wore trousers that were embroidered with seahorses and starfish, and her boots were made from shiny turtle leather.

"Ah, my precious little Petticoat Pirates,

I'm so pleased you're back safely from your adventures."

The Captainess took off her riding hat. Her red hair was twisted into a bun on the back of her head and secured with a starfish clasp.

"You are all truly courageous pirates and I am proud to call you my own," she said, putting her arms around the girls and gathering them together. "Now, Marina, are you ready?"

"Yes, Captainess," Marina said. She stood up straight and put on her own riding hat – her long black hair was also swept back into a plaited bun.

"Here, let us help." Aqua and Oceana both tucked Marina's loose curls under her hat.

"Good luck – we'll be watching and cheering you on!" they said as Marina walked out of the cabin door with the Captainess. They

headed to the side of *The Petticoat* where Misty was tethered. The Captainess's beautiful blue seahorse, Oyster-Star, was waiting there too.

The pair rode their seahorses into Periwinkle Lagoon's calm waters. The rocks around the lagoon were beginning to fill up with spectators who were all cheering as the showjumping teams paraded around and practised in the water.

"Look, over there," Marina said to the Captainess. "There's Queen Olinda, and her sister Luna."

"Ah yes. We gave them two of our finest seahorses early this morn. They seem to be very able riders," the Captainess said, winking at Marina.

Marina waved at Queen Olinda and Luna as they rode past on white seahorses. The

Jellyfish Queen bowed her head solemnly, but Luna looked away.

Suddenly the pirate trumpeters started up – the gala was about to begin. Marina's tummy felt as though it were filled with jumping sea beans!

"Marina!" she heard faint voices call from above her. It was Aqua and Oceana. They'd

been invited to sit in the royal box with the Ice Queen and King who had come to present the trophy for the grand race.

Marina felt much better knowing her friends were there to support her.

The competition began. The crowd gasped and clapped as various teams jumped out of the water over driftwood bars before splashing back down again, still mounted on their seahorses.

Soon it was Marina's and the Captainess's turn to jump. Marina looked at the three high driftwood bars that were floating ahead of her. In unison, Marina and the Captainess charged forward on their seahorses, leaping out of the water and over the bars. The crowd clapped wildly as they both sploshed back down into the water perfectly.

Next it was Queen Olinda's turn. She nodded to Luna before they too charged forward together, clearing the bars with elegance and poise. The crowd cheered.

After some more rounds of jumping it was time to announce the finalists.

The Ice Queen stepped forward and called out the names of the two teams who would be competing against each other in the grand race.

"Would the following teams ride forward to me!" she shouted in a booming voice. "The Jellyfish team from Scallop Bay."

Marina looked at Captainess Periwinkle nervously, crossing her fingers that they were in the final too.

"And," the Queen continued, "Captainess Periwinkle and Marina from Periwinkle Lagoon."

The crowd whooped and stomped as the two teams rode up to face the Queen and King who were now holding the Ice Pearl Trophy up for everyone to see.

"Teams," the King said, "this competition has been held in the waters of Periwinkle Lagoon for many hundreds of years. This magical trophy is bestowed upon the team

who are deemed the best seahorse riders. Ride fairly, for the Ice Pearl will know if you are not being an honest rider. Only the true and fair will benefit from the trophy's magical powers."

Marina smiled again at Queen Olinda and Luna. Luna looked away for a moment but then looked back at Marina and smiled too.

"Riders, take your places please."

Marina's hands shook slightly as she held Misty's reins tightly. The grand race was the most difficult and only very skilled riders would be able to finish the course.

Marina and Captainess Periwinkle went first. They jumped over four driftwood bars, and then swam in and out of coral poles. Next the pair had to raise the seahorses out of the water by unfurling their tails and then push a sea urchin off the top of a post with

the seahorses' snouts. The crowd watched in complete silence.

The final obstacle was a grand ring of ice that they had to jump through together. Marina looked at the Captainess and they nodded to one another before bravely charging towards the frozen ring.

Both Marina and the Captainess jumped much, much higher than either of them ever had before! As they landed safely on the other side the Ice Queen called out their time. "One minute and forty-five seconds."

"Wow," Marina said, out of breath, "I've never jumped so high in my life!"

Captainess Periwinkle smiled proudly at her Petticoat Pirate.

It was now the turn of Queen Olinda and Luna. The spectators watched nervously as the

pair made their way around the same obstacles. Finally they jumped through the ring of ice with the same grace and elegance as Marina and the Captainess.

"One minute and forty-five seconds!" the Ice Queen called out.

"A draw!" Marina gasped, turning to the Captainess. "What happens now?"

"Listen, my good pirate, and you will find out," said Captainess Periwinkle with a smile.

The Ice Queen and Ice King stepped forward together, holding the Ice Pearl Trophy high up above their heads. "In the event of a draw," the King called out, "the Ice Pearl will decide who is the worthy winner."

Marina and the Captainess, Queen Olinda and Luna rode up in front of the royal box. They

watched in awe as the large pearly trophy began to glow brightly. It lifted away from the King's and Queen's hands and floated down in front of the Seahorse Gala competitors. It glowed brighter and brighter and grew bigger and bigger until there was suddenly a large flash of white.

Marina looked down. There in her hand was the trophy! She looked over to Queen Olinda, and she was holding a trophy too. The Ice Pearl had split itself into two! Marina and Olinda looked at one another in astonishment.

"Not in all my years have I ever seen that happen!" the Captainess exclaimed. She

turned to Queen Olinda and Luna. "We will hold a grand feast to celebrate, and we would be honoured if you'd stay and join us in our joint victory."

"Thank you, you're most kind, Captainess Periwinkle," said Queen Olinda. "But we are eager to return home now to Scallop Bay. We are very grateful that you allowed us to take part in your gala." And at that, Queen Olinda and Luna rode back to their galleon.

"Well," Captainess Periwinkle said to Marina, "that's the first time I've ever met Jellyfish people."

"And I think it will be the last," Marina whispered to herself.

Chapter Ten

Grand dining floats were sailed into the lagoon, decorated with bunting and balloons, and laden with delicious treats.

Meanwhile, Aqua and Oceana had joined Marina, the Captainess and the Ice King and Queen in the royal box.

"Well done, Marina, we're so proud of you!" said Oceana, throwing her arms around her friend.

"And you look a-m-a-z-i-n-g," Aqua added

as Marina let down her raven locks and plopped her riding hat down on the table.

The grand old Ice King walked over to the girls. "Well done, young lady," he boomed. "Why I've not seen riding as good as that in many years!"

"Thank you," Marina said, holding on to

her friends' hands. "But I couldn't have done it without the support of my friends. We've been through a lot together."

"Yes, I hear you had quite the adventure at Scallop Bay. Nasty things those salt spiders." He tapped his nose to show he understood and then wandered back to his enormous plate of seafood.

"I wonder if Queen Olinda has arrived home yet. I hope she feels more confident as a Queen now," Marina said.

"And feels like she can stand up to that bossy little sister of hers!" Aqua added.

Suddenly there was a flap and a squawk as a large seagull landed clumsily on Marina's shoulder and almost made her spill her sea cherryade. It was a sea-post gull!

"Well that wasn't very elegant!" Marina

laughed as the bird passed her a letter out of its satchel with its beak.

Marina opened the letter, which had the scallop emblem of the Jellyfish people at the top.

"It's from Queen Olinda!" she said, unfolding the shimmery piece of paper.

Dear Marina, Aqua and Oceana,
I am writing to you from my galleon on

my voyage home to Scallop Bay.

As you well know, we, the Jellyfish people, are very private, and do not wish to mix with the sea people around us. But it has been a blessing to have met you three Petticoat Pirates. Never would I have imagined that three young girls could display such bravery to help their people, and in turn helping mine.

We here at Scallop Bay will never change our ways — we like our island home, protected by the mists and salt spiders. I would like you to know however, that you will always be most welcome to visit us anytime you choose.

I have regained the respect of my

people and I hope that I can learn to be the Queen they deserve. I am going to put Luna in charge of our seahorses, which I think she will enjoy very much!

Your friend for ever,

Queen Olinda

Marina pressed the letter close to her chest and a little tear of happiness fell from her eye.

Her two friends lay their heads on Marina's shoulders as they quietly whispered, "May the Petticoat Pirates prevail!"

The three pirates clinked their cups of sea cherryade. "To our next adventure!" they cheered. "Wherever that may be!"

The End

Ship's Log

Now that you've learnt all about Marina,
Aqua and Oceana, why not read on to see
how you can have a Petticoat Pirate
adventure of your own!

Petticoat Pirate Lexicon

Would you like to speak like a proper Petticoat Pirate? Of course you would!

Captainess	*The queen of the pirates*
Cabin	*A room on board a ship*
Foolish as a flapper fish	*The way you feel when you've done something silly*
Galleon	*A large and impressive pirate ship*
Mother of pearl	*A really pretty, shiny material found on the inside of some shells. It's also very strong, so Oceana's glasses are made from this!*

Narwhal swords	*Long, swirled sticks made from the horns of the narwhal – a whale which is sometimes known as the unicorn of the sea*
Port	*Left*
Porthole	*A little round window on a ship*
Sea cherryade	*A delicious fizzy drink made from sea cherries*
Sea-post gull	*A seagull who has been specially trained to deliver pirate post*
Sea sugar cubes	*A sugary treat, loved by seahorses*
Starboard	*Right*
Sticky situation	*A difficult or worrying situation*
Tentacles	*Jellyfish (and octopuses) have these instead of arms or legs – they use them to feel and to draw in food*
Wind whisper	*The way Marina talks to the wind. The wind always tells the truth, but sometimes it's hard to understand the messages it carries*

May the Petticoat Pirates prevail!

We wish the Petticoat Pirates strength and success!

Make Your Own Petticoat Pirate Hat

The best way to look like a real pirate is to make yourself a pirate hat, just like the ones Marina, Aqua and Oceana wear! (You might need a little bit of help from a grown-up for this activity.)

What you will need

- A piece of card or thick sugar paper (you can choose any colour you like – the girls all have black hats)

- Thin white paper, or tracing paper
- Scissors, sticky tape and glue
- A piece of elastic
- Any decorations you like – for example sequins and glitter

What to do

1. Trace or photocopy the image overleaf and cut it out.

2. Place the shape on your piece of card and draw around it. Then, very carefully flip it over and draw around it again – now you'll have a full hat shape.

3. Cut out the hat shape and decorate the front with anything you like! Marina has a heart shape on her hat, Aqua has a star and Oceana has a seahorse.

4. Bend the hat so the ends meet, and use sticky tape to secure them together. This part can be tricky so you might need help!

5. Use some more sticky tape to fasten your elastic to each side so that you have a loop to keep the hat on your head.

6. Wear your hat at a jaunty angle just like the Petticoat Pirates!

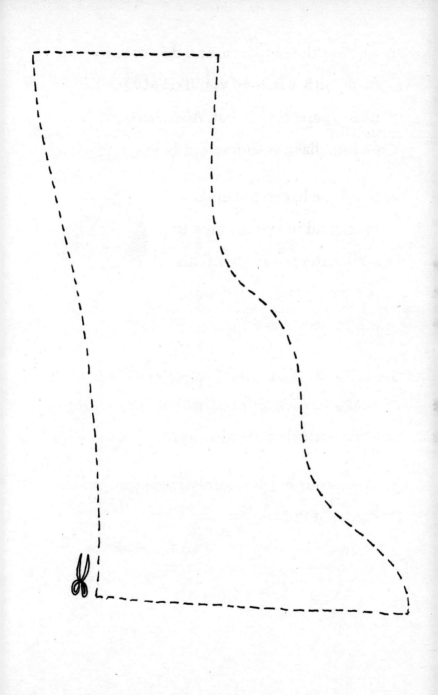

The Petticoat

Can you guess which cabin belongs to which Petticoat Pirate?

Scallop Bay Maze

Can you help the Petticoat Pirates get safely through the forest and find the Jellyfish Queen's castle?

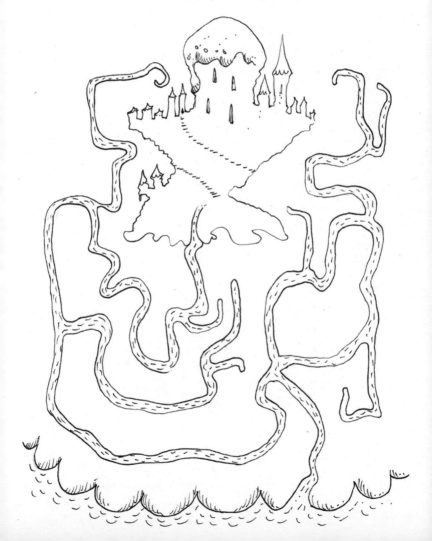